John Bright

The Rt. Hon. John Bright, M. P.

John Bright

The Rt. Hon. John Bright, M. P.

ISBN/EAN: 9783337163457

Printed in Europe, USA, Canada, Australia, Japan

Cover: Foto ©Raphael Reischuk / pixelio.de

More available books at **www.hansebooks.com**

THE RT. HON.

JOHN BRIGHT

M.P.

Cartoons from the Collection of

" Mʀ· PUNCH."

NCH OFFICE, 85, FLEET STREET, LONDON.

1878.

The Rt. Hon. John Bright,
M.P.

SON of Jacob Bright, of Greenbank, Rochdale, Lancashire; born in 1811; one of the firm of John Bright and Brothers, cotton spinners and manufacturers, Rochdale; a member of the Society of Friends; joined the Anti-Corn-Law League soon after its formation in 1838, and, with Mr. Cobden, became one of its leading members, and the powerful champion of Free Trade; returned to Parliament for the city of Durham in 1843, and continued to sit as its representative till 1847, when he was elected for Manchester; opposed the war with Russia, 1854; rejected at Manchester at the General Election in 1857, consequent on the defeat of Lord Palmerston's Government on the China question; returned for Birmingham the same year, and is still member for that constituency; the great advocate of Free Trade, Financial Reform, a wide extension of the Suffrage, a redistribution of Seats and the Ballot, of the cause of Ireland and India, of National Education, and of Peace; in the American Civil War took the Anti-Slavery side, and was the staunch supporter of the Northern States; visited Ireland in 1866; accepted a post in Mr. Gladstone's Cabinet in 1868 as President of the Board of Trade—the state of his health prevented him from undertaking the duties of the India Office—when he was nominated a Privy Councillor ; resigned office at the end of 1870; on his health becoming more satisfactory, he returned to the Gladstone Cabinet in 1873, as Chancellor of the Duchy of Lancaster, but retired with his colleagues at the beginning of the following year.

Mr. Bright is one of the most eloquent and effective orators of his time, and his speeches were collected and published in 1868; the policy which he has for so many years advocated has in most points been in the end accepted by the nation.

A LIST OF THE CARTOONS.

THE RT. HON.

JOHN BRIGHT,

M.P.

CARTOONS FROM "PUNCH."

1846—1875.

C——N.   SIR R. P——L.   B——T.

THE SEVEN-LEAGUE BOOTS;

OR, DEATH OF GIANT MONOPOLY.

☞ The labours of Messrs. Cobden and Bright procured the recognition of Free Trade principles, and, with Sir Robert Peel, extorted from a reluctant Parliament the repeal of the Corn Laws.—1846.

No. 1.

A *BRIGHT* IDEA.

THE PEACE RECRUITING SERGEANT TRYING TO ENLIST THE DUKE.

☞ Mr. Bright's peace principles were embodied in the plan proposed this year to settle all international differences by arbitration. The scheme was not viewed with much favour.—1849.

No. 2.

"NOT QUITE SUCH A FINE CHILD AS THE LAST!"

☞ Lord John Russell's second Reform Bill was coldly received by Mr. Bright and other ardent reformers. The Ministry fell shortly after its introduction, and the measure was never discussed.—1852.

EATING THE LEEK.

FLUELLEN . . . MR. COBDEN.   PISTOL . . . MR. DISRAELI.

FLUELLEN. "*I pray you fall to; if you can mock a leek, you can eat a leek.*"—HEN. V.

☞ The Derby Ministry declared their adherence to the Free-trade Policy of Messrs. Cobden and Bright, which they had formerly resisted.—1852.

No. 4.

PET OF THE MANCHESTER SCHOOL.

" He shall have a little Turk to pull to pieces—that he shall."

☞ Messrs. Bright and Cobden incurred much odium by their persistent opposition to the Anti-Russian feeling of the nation at the outbreak of the Crimean war.—1854.

No. 5.

B——T.   G——E.   D——I.

THE NEW COALITION.

☞ Messrs. Bright, Gladstone, and Disraeli were, at this time (though for different reasons) in accord in their opposition to Lord Palmerston's Government.—1855.

No. 6.

No. 7.

RECOIL OF THE GREAT CHINESE GUN-TRICK.

☞ Mr. Bright was rejected at Manchester on Lord Palmerston's appeal to the country after his defeat by Mr. Cobden on the China Question. He was shortly afterwards returned for Birmingham without opposition.—1857.

ORESTES PURSUED BY THE FURIES.

"IT WILL SOON BOIL!"

☞ The constituencies at this time were apathetic on the Reform Question. Mr. Bright had been addressing numerous Meetings to elicit popular support.—1858.

No. 9.

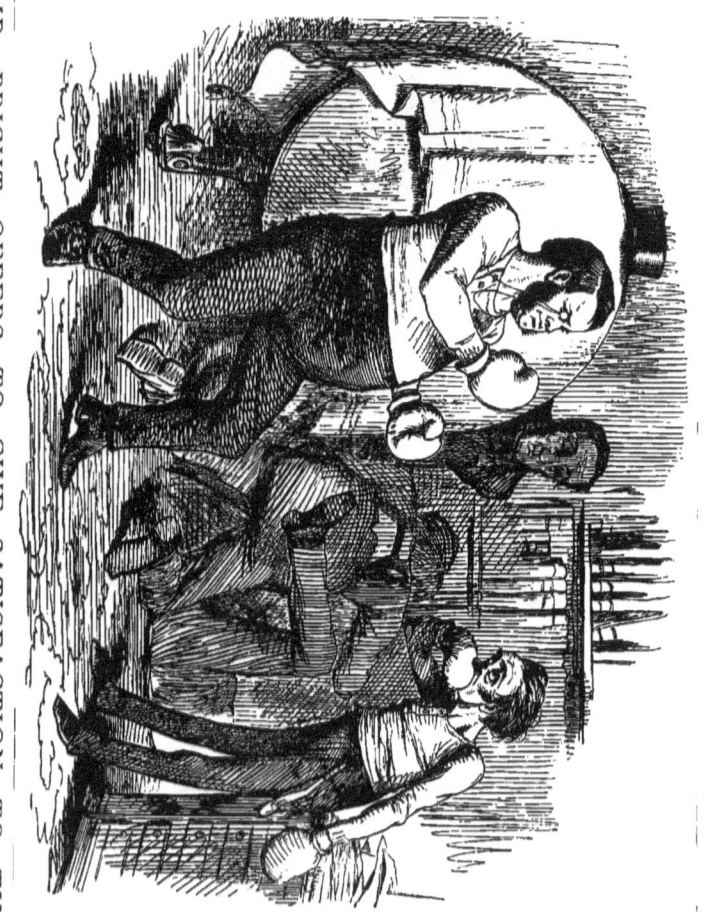

MR. BRIGHT OFFERS TO GIVE SATISFACTION TO THE LIBERAL PARTY.

☞ Mr. Bright rejected the timid Reform proposals of the Whigs, and demanded the widest extension of the franchise.—1858.

A VERY GREASY POLE.

☞ Mr. Bright had been addressing large Meetings in the manufacturing districts to agitate for an extension of the franchise to all rated householders.—1859.

No. 11.

THE QUAKER AND THE BAUBLE.

*"It is the Land which the territorial party represents in Parliament. * * * That is the theory of the Constitution:* BLACKSTONE *says so. But it is a thing which is not likely to be respected much longer, and it must go, even if involving the destruction of the Constitution."*—MR. BRIGHT, *in his Penny Organ.*

☞ The "Morning Star"—a journal founded to advocate the views of Mr. Bright—met with little support. After an uncertain existence of some years, it was discontinued.—1859.

No. 12.

WHO WILL ROUSE HIM?

☞ Mr. Bright's pertinacious demand for a Reform Bill, and the endeavours of both political parties to settle the question, failed to awaken the indifference of the constituencies.—1859.

THE REAL UGLY RUSH.

" He feared there would be an ugly rush some of these days."—MR. HENLEY on the Reform Bill.

☞ The Reform Question had become for both parties a battle ground for the possession of the Treasury bench. It proved fatal to the Derby Ministry in the preceding month.—1859.

No. 14.

THE REFORM JANUS.

☞ Lord John Russell's new Reform proposals, though framed with great care, again failed to receive Mr. Bright's approval, and were at the same time distasteful to the Conservative Party.—1860.

BRIGHT THE PEACE-MAKER.

☞ Mr. Bright took an active part in supporting the repeal of the Paper Duty. He condemned the action of the Upper House in rejecting the Bill, and charged them with usurping the powers properly belonging to the Commons.—1860.

DISSENT IN EARNEST.

" We defer to their feelings, but we cannot assent to their reasoning."—PARL. DEBATE.

☞ Mr. Bright's forcible opposition influenced the Government in withdrawing from the Census Bill the invidious clause relating to the Statistics of Religious Denominations.—1860.

COBDEN'S LOGIC.

"*I don't know, perhaps, any country in the world where the* MASSES OF THE PEOPLE ARE SO ILLITERATE AS IN ENGLAND. * * * *Sound Statesmanship requires such an extension of the franchise as shall admit the Masses of the People to political power.*"—FROM MR. COBDEN'S Speech at Rochdale.

☞ This speech gave occasion to much angry comment, and led to a personal dispute between Mr. Cobden and the Editor of the *Times.*—1863.

No. 18.

DR. BRIGHT AND HIS PATIENT.

DOCTOR. "*Do you get good wages?*"
PATIENT. "*Yes.*"
DOCTOR. "*Have you plenty to eat and drink?*"
PATIENT. "*Yes, as far as that goes.*"
DOCTOR. "*Do you do as you like?*"
PATIENT. "*Yes.*"
DOCTOR. "*Do you pay taxes?*"
PATIENT. "*None to hurt me much.*"
DOCTOR. "*Ah! We must change all that. We must go in for REFORM!*"

☞ This colloquy gives a not unfair summary of Mr. Bright's address to his constituents in the preceding month.—1865.

No. 19.

THE POLITICAL "WALL-FLOWER."

MISS BRIGHT. *"Nobody asks Me; and if they did, I should certainly decline."*

☞ Lord Russell's Whig prejudices were too strong to permit his offering Mr. Bright a seat in the Cabinet—though none had better deserved it.—1865.

No. 20.

JOHN SLOW AND JOHN FAST.

EARL RUSSELL. " *Well, well! Don't be violent, Mr. Bright, and proper inquiries shall be made, as we have perfect confidence in our friend, Mr. Workingman.*"

☞ Lord Russell claimed to have a monopoly of the Reform Question, and was not prepared to make the violent changes demanded by Mr. Bright.—1865.

No. 21.

SCENE FROM ST. STEPHEN'S PANTOMIME.

Clown (Mr. Bright). "*What a beautiful child! Let me take care of it for yer, mum.*"

☞ The Ministry were deaf alike to Mr. Bright's menaces and persuasions, and their Bill, as ultimately framed, did not contain any of the points for which he contended.—1865.

No. 22.

THE OFFICIOUS PASSENGER.

Lord John. "*Excuse me, friend Bright, but do you command this ship, or do I ?*"

☞ Mr. Bright not having been admitted to the Cabinet, was endeavouring from the platform to force the hands of the Ministry.—1866.

No. 23.

GOING DOWN TO THE HOUSE.

LORD RUSSELL. "*Well, Bright, what do* YOU *want ?*"
JOHNNY BRIGHT. "*Anything your Honour is willing to give me* NOW."

☞ Mr. Bright was now prepared to accept any reduction of the franchise—being convinced that neither the Ministry nor Parliament would agree to a Radical measure.—1866.

No. 24.

THE BRUMMAGEM FRANKENSTEIN.

JOHN BRIGHT. *"I have no fe—fe—fear of ma—manhood suffrage!"*

[MR. BRIGHT'S Speech at Birmingham.

☞ The unwillingness of Parliament to accept any measure of Reform had aroused a wide-spread discontent
amongst the working classes. A monster gathering was held at Birmingham in August.—1866.

No. 25.

THE POPULAR POLL-PARROT.

PARROT SONG. *"Pretty democra—a—ats! Take 'em to the poll! Naughty Bob*
Lowe! Schgree—e—e—yx!!!"

☞ Mr. Bright was now addressing Reform Meetings in various towns. The burden of them was—an abuse
of Mr. Lowe, who had aided in rejecting Lord Russell's measure.—1866.

No. 26.

DR. DULCAMARA IN DUBLIN.

☞ Mr. Bright visited Dublin, by request, in October. His speeches were mainly devoted to the discussion of Irish questions.—1866.

THE FESTIVE SEASON.
(A Pleasant, but we fear a somewhat Improbable, Picture.)

Mr. B * * * *, M.P. "*I shay Lowe, old f'la, lesh shwear 'ternal fr'en'ship!*"
Mr. L * * *, M.P. "*All right, Johnny. Been boshe in the wrong.*"

☞ Not so improbable after all. Within two years from this date Messrs. Bright and Lowe were colleagues
in the same Cabinet.—1866.

No. 28.

RIVAL SWEEPERS.

GENERAL CHORUS. *"Clear yer door-step down, mum?"*

☞ All parties were pledged to a renewal of the Reform discussion in the approaching Session. There was, therefore, every prospect of an animated rivalry.—1867.

No. 29.

DR. BULL'S WAITING-ROOM.

BENJAMIN (*to* HIBERNIA). "*Please 'm, the doctor'll take your case just 'm.*"

☞ Mr. Bright's further agitation of the Reform Question was (for the present) arrested by that of the Irish Church, which was uppermost in the minds of the country.—1868.

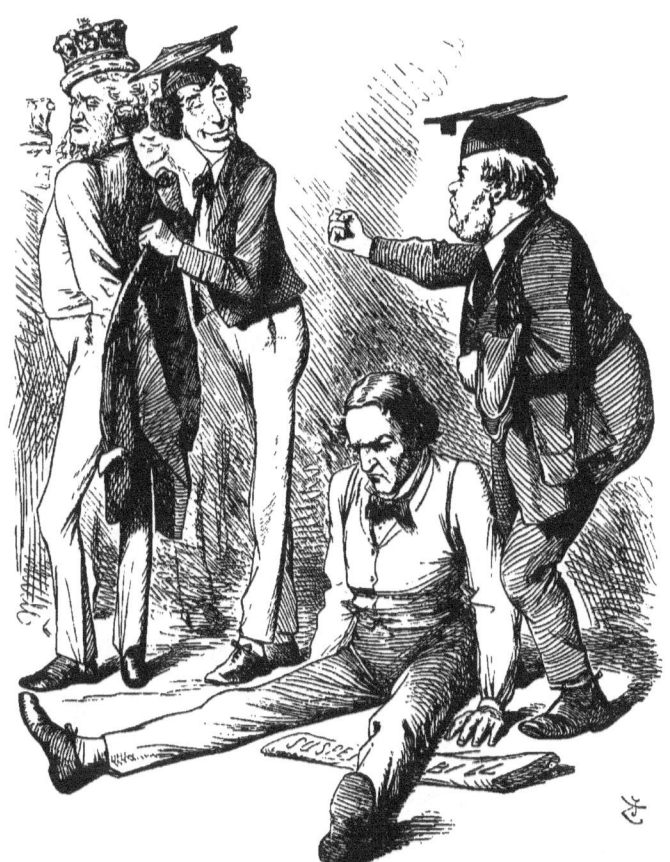

ATHLETICS AT WESTMINSTER.

JOHN BRIGHT. "*Ha! Won't you ketch it next half, when our big brother comes ! ! !*"

☞ Mr. Gladstone's Irish Church Suspensory Bill was thrown out by the Lords. The "big brother" was the Borough constituencies enlarged by the New Reform Bill.—1868.

No. 32.

A DRESS REHEARSAL.

FRIEND BRIGHT. *"H'm! Ha! Verily these Ministerial garments won't be so unbecoming, after all!"*

[Said, in other words, in his last address.]

☞ The Leadership of the Liberal Party having escaped from the hands of the Whigs, made it more than probable that Mr. Bright would have a seat in their next Cabinet.—1868.

No. 33.

A "FRIEND" AT COURT.

WHAT WE HAVE READ. "*Mr. Bright attended yesterday at Windsor, and kissed Her Majesty's hand on his appointment to the Board of Trade.*"

☞ The defeat of the Conservatives at the General Election was followed by the formation of a Liberal Administration, in which Mr. Bright was included as President of the Board of Trade.—1868.

No. 34.

"REJECTED!"

OR, THE VICISSITUDES OF *ART*.

☞ Mr. Bright's long advocacy of the Irish Church Disestablishment, after being in principle rejected alike by all Administrations, was now successfully realized.—1869.

No. 35.

FORGETTING HIS PLACE.

JOHN BRIGHT. "*Irish Church coming down!—pull out o' the way there with that 'infatuated' old machine of yours —can't yer?*"

GROOM OF THE CHAMBERS. "*John, John, you're* FORGETTING YOUR PLACE—*you mustn't use that sort of language* NOW."

☞ Mr. Bright's characteristic disregard of the Upper House had been unwisely expressed in a published letter to his constituents.—1869.

No. 36.

JOHN BRIGHT'S NEW REFORM BILL.--
"REFORM YOURSELVES!"

☞ Mr. Bright addressed his constituents on the evils of the Liquor traffic; urging, that it was a question—
not for Government, but for themselves.—1870.

No. 37.

THE BILL OF FARE.

MR. GLADSTONE (THE "CHIEF"). "*Irish stew first, Mrs. B., and then——*"

MRS. BRIGHT (THE COOK). "*Lor bless you, Mr. G., the Irish stew's quite as much as they'll get through, I'll be bound!*"

☞ Commenting on the difficulty of passing several important measures in one Session, Mr. Bright had said, "It was not easy to drive six omnibuses abreast through Temple Bar."—1870.

No. 38.

"OFF GREENWICH."

JOHN BRIGHT. "*Come aboard, sir!*"

CAPTAIN GLADSTONE. "*Glad to see you, John. Glad you're A.B. again. If it comes on to blow, we may want your assistance.*"

☞ Mr. Bright had withdrawn from the Ministry on account of ill-health. His re-appearance in Parliament tended to strengthen the now weakened Administration.—1872.

A FRIEND IN NEED.

Mr. Gladstone. *"My dear John, I congratulate you! Just in time to settle accounts with our black friend yonder!"*
John Bright. *"H'm! Fighting is not quite in my line, at that knowcut, friend William; nevertheless—!"*

☞ Several important changes had been made with the view of strengthening the Cabinet. Amongst others, Mr. Bright again accepted office as Chancellor of the Duchy of Lancaster. The Ashantee War was now in progress.—1873.

THE NEW SHEPHERD.

HARTINGTON (*new hand, just taken on*). "*Hey, but measter !*—WHERE BE THE SHEEP ?"

☞ Mr. Bright's nomination of Lord Hartington as Leader of the shattered Liberal Party was acquiesced in by the rival candidates.—1875.